This book belongs to:

The Bug Hunt

Disney's Out & About With Pooh
A Grow and Learn Library

Published by Advance Publishers
© 1996 Disney Enterprises, Inc.
Based on the Pooh stories by A. A. Milne © The Pooh Properties Trust.

Written by Ann Braybrooks
Illustrated by Arkadia Illustration Ltd.
Designed by Vickey Bolling
Produced by Bumpy Slide Books

ISBN:1-885222-71-8
10 9 8 7 6 5 4

One warm summer day, Pooh and his friends were relaxing after a picnic. "Did I ever tell you about my Aunt Augusta?" said Owl. "She was a lepidopterist."

"A what?" asked Pooh, lazily licking the rim of a honey pot.

"A butterfly collector," said Owl. "She collected butterflies — like that wonderful specimen over there."

"Speci-what?" said Pooh.

As Owl pointed to the colorful insect, Roo jumped up and ran after it.

"I can catch it!" he cried. "Watch me!"

But when Roo tried to grab the butterfly, it flitted away.

"That's all right, Roo," said Owl. "I can teach you how to be a bug collector."

"I know!" said Christopher Robin. "Let's all go on a bug hunt together!"

The friends agreed that a bug hunt was a splendid idea. Owl puffed up his chest feathers and said, "Pooh, you wash the empty jars in the stream. If we catch something, Kanga can poke holes in the paper from our sandwiches and put it over the jars. That way, the bugs can breathe. Now, as for butterfly nets . . . "

"I have some at home," Christopher Robin offered. "I'll go get them."

As Christopher Robin ran off, Owl spied Eeyore still resting beneath a tree. "Eeyore!" Owl cried. "Why aren't you helping?"

"Me?" asked Eeyore sleepily. "Eating all that thistle made

me drowsy. I'll stay here and watch our things. Pooh has one honey pot left. I wouldn't want a heffalump to get it."

"Oh, all right," muttered Owl, shaking his head.

A while later Christopher Robin returned, and the friends divided up the jars and butterfly nets. As Tigger slung his net over his shoulder, he proclaimed, "Bug hunting is what Tiggers do best!"

So Roo begged to go bug-hunting with Tigger, and Piglet quickly chose Pooh for a partner. Christopher Robin and Kanga paired off, which left Rabbit to team up with Owl. Eeyore remained under the tree.

As the friends scattered in different directions, Tigger said, "C'mon, Roo. I know a place that's full of bugs. Big bugs. Little bugs. Polka-dotted bugs. Bugs that are striped, like me!"

Soon Tigger and Roo arrived at the meadow. "I don't see any bugs," said Roo.

"Shh," said Tigger, stepping carefully. "They're hiding."

Suddenly a large green bug leaped out of the grass.

"A grasshopper!" cried Roo. "Catch it!"

Tigger swung the net but missed.

"I know," said Tigger, "if you hop about in the grass,

you might startle the grasshopper, and it will leap out."

Sure enough, as Roo hopped about in the grass, the startled grasshopper jumped into view. Tigger swung his net. "I caught it!" he cried. "What did I tell you?"

Meanwhile, Owl and Rabbit had not journeyed far from the picnic spot. Instead of catching bugs, they were arguing. As they stood on the path, Rabbit said, "I know we'll find more bugs at the Floody Place."

Owl said, "I'm sure we'll find more bugs at the Six Pine Trees."

"The Floody Place," argued Rabbit.

"The Six Pine Trees," insisted Owl.

At the same time, Christopher Robin and Kanga were trying to catch dragonflies. Each time Christopher Robin swung the net, the darting insects escaped across the pond.

Finally, Christopher Robin said, "Perhaps if you hold onto my shirt, Kanga, I can reach a little farther."

As Kanga dug her feet into the ground, the boy swung his net. When he felt himself falling, he cried, "Kanga, let go!" But he was too late. Kanga tumbled in after him.

As they climbed out of the water, Kanga glanced at the net. "Oh, my," she said. "We caught one!"

Meanwhile, Owl and Rabbit were *still* arguing. Rabbit said, "I say we draw twigs. Whoever picks the longer twig wins."

"But who's going to hold the twigs?" Owl asked. "If I hold them, you might think I'm cheating. And if *you* hold them, well . . . I still say we should look for bugs at the Six Pine Trees."

"I say the Floody Place!" cried Rabbit.

Off in the woods, Pooh and Piglet were searching for sow bugs.

As they crouched down near a log, Piglet asked, "If we don't find any sow bugs, are we going to look for bees?"

"No," said Pooh. "Bees would not like being in a jar.

We'll let the bees be."

Piglet giggled at Pooh's rhyme. Then he grew serious. "But Pooh, what if we find something else that stings?" he asked.

"Don't worry," said Pooh. "Most bugs are harmless."

When the friends didn't find any sow bugs, they continued their search.

A while later, Piglet saw a caterpillar crawling on a milkweed leaf. "We could capture *that*," he said.

"We could," said Pooh, thinking. "But what if the caterpillar makes a cocoon around itself? Does a cocoon count as a bug?"

"I don't know," said Piglet. "But there's one right there."

As Pooh gazed at the delicate sack, he said, "Where there are caterpillars and cocoons, there must be butterflies, too. That's what caterpillars turn into after they're all done being in their cocoon."

Pooh and Piglet sat down to watch for butterflies, but soon their eyelids began to droop. As the friends dozed, a dozen butterflies danced around them, flashing their orange and black wings.

Meanwhile, Owl and Rabbit had not budged. After hours of bickering, Owl finally said, "I give up. We'll try the Floody Place."

Triumphant at last, Rabbit ran down the path. Owl followed behind.

As they passed Rabbit's garden, Owl exclaimed, "My word! Look at all the ladybugs!"

Owl thrust the net at Rabbit and grabbed the jar. Then he ran into the garden and began scooping the bright red bugs into its mouth.

Rabbit rushed after Owl. "No, no, no!" Rabbit cried. "Don't touch my ladybugs!"

Rabbit reached for the jar, but Owl refused to let go.

"Give it to me!" Rabbit yelled.

"No!" cried Owl. "I need it to catch the ladybugs!"

"No, you don't!" Rabbit sputtered, "*I* need the ladybugs for my garden. Ladybugs eat the pesty bugs that chew up my plants!"

As Owl let go of the jar, Rabbit lurched backward. "Oof!"
he said, landing in some lettuce. "Now look what you did!"
"I'm sorry," said Owl. "Truly. But where are all the pests

you were telling me about? I don't see anything but ladybugs."

Rabbit sat up and looked around. "Neither do I," he said cheerfully. "The ladybugs must have eaten them all."

As Rabbit stood up and dusted himself off, he noticed his shadow. "Goodness gracious," he said. "It's late. We'd better go back."

As Owl and Rabbit hurried along, Owl said, "How embarrassing! We didn't catch any bugs."

"And whose fault is that?" Rabbit asked.

"Not mine!" cried Owl.

When Rabbit and Owl arrived at the picnic spot, Christopher Robin heard them arguing.

"You silly things," said Christopher Robin. "Have you been bickering all this time?"

"No," said Rabbit.

"Yes," said Owl.

Roo bounced up and asked, "Did you catch anything? Tigger and I caught a grasshopper!"

"We caught a dragonfly," said Kanga.

"And we found a butterfly!" cried Pooh. "Rather, it found us. It flew into the jar while we were resting."

Just then Eeyore discovered that he had caught
something, too. "Ants," he said. "On Pooh's honey pot."
Rabbit threw down his net. "That does it!" he exclaimed.

"Even Eeyore caught something! Owl, we were foolish. If we hadn't spent all that time arguing, we might have caught some bugs."

"You're right," said Owl. "For once we agree!"

"At last!" Rabbit chuckled.

Dusk fell, and the collectors lifted the napkins off their jars and let the bugs go. Moments later, tiny flashing lights twinkled before their eyes.

"Fireflies!" exclaimed Christopher Robin.

As a gentle breeze rustled the grass, the friends sat back and enjoyed the amazing light show that seemed meant just for them.